R___ was stirring a potion in a glass rose
b___ while Hope read from a book and added
t___ agments of petals to the bowl.

"Oh, look," said Merry, "there's Ruth and
H___."

"That's odd," said Gabrielle. "Ruth said she
h___ asses of reading to do. And Hope said
s___ as going to visit Perdita at the stables."

"Oh, I wonder what they're doing?" said

"Yes, I wonder," said Gabrielle.

First published in the UK in 2013 by Usborne Publishing Ltd.,
Usborne House, 83-85 Saffron Hill, London EC1N 8RT, England.
www.usborne.com

Copyright © Janey Louise Jones, 2013

The right of Janey Louise Jones to be identified as the author of this work has been
asserted by her in accordance with the Copyright, Designs and Patents Act, 1988.

Illustrations by Antonia Miller.
Illustrations copyright © Usborne Publishing Ltd., 2013

The name Usborne and the devices ⊕ ⊕ are Trade Marks of Usborne Publishing Ltd.

This is a work of fiction. The characters, incidents, and dialogues are products of
the author's imagination and are not to be construed as real. Any resemblance
to actual events or persons, living or dead, is entirely coincidental.

A CIP catalogue record for this book is available from the British Library.

JFMAMJJA OND/13  ISBN 9781409538622  02788/1
Printed in Reading, Berkshire, UK.

# Friendship and Flowers

## Janey Louise Jones

USBORNE

Chapter 1

"I'm back!" Gabrielle cried, as she burst through the door of the room she shared with her three friends at Angel Academy.

"Gabrielle!" exclaimed her friends excitedly.

"Oh, it's so good to see you!" she said, as they all embraced in a lovely huddle.

It was the beginning of the spring term and Gabrielle Divine was delighted to be back at school in the angel world on Cloud Nimbus.

"How was Christmas on earth?" asked Ruth Bell, her red curls bobbing around her freckly cheeks. Ruth had been Gabrielle's best friend since their first day at Angel Academy.

"It was lovely to be home with Mum and Dad, but I missed you all so much!"

Gabrielle was unique on Cloud Nimbus as an Earth Angel, with both human and angel genes. She'd been invited to Angel Academy, a school in a beautiful white chateau, to become a Cherubic – a trainee Guardian Angel – and she'd already spent a term there. Going back to earth for Christmas *had* been great fun, but she had missed her angel friends and her angel horse, Domino, very much.

"And we missed you loads!" said Hope Honeychurch, another of Gabrielle's room-mates and the twin sister of Charity. "Especially when we all met up in the holidays and you weren't there!"

"Hope's right. It wasn't the same without you, Gabrielle," said Charity. "Four is much more fun than three." Gabrielle, Ruth, Hope and Charity all shared the Crystals dormitory, and Gabrielle thought they made a perfect team. And of course there was Sylvie too. Sylvie was the girls' gorgeous pink and silver dove, who ran messages for them and watched over them from the windowsill. She fluttered into the room to greet Gabrielle.

"Welcome! It's lovely to see you again, and you look so well!" chirped Sylvie.

"Oh, Sylvie! It's wonderful to see you again too! What have you been doing in the holidays?" A talking dove no longer surprised Gabrielle, though it had when they'd first met.

"I've been helping the teachers with the new timetables and taking messages between the stables and the school," Sylvie said.

"Wow! I wonder what we'll be learning this term!" said Charity, who loved to be organized and was always eager to learn the details of school life so she could plan ahead in her diary. It was a Sunday, which meant that lessons would begin the next morning.

"Wait until your teachers tell you," said Sylvie. "All I will say is that in the first two weeks there will be lots of Potion-making, so that you can take your Vanishing Charm test very soon!"

"Oh, I can't wait!" said Gabrielle. "Imagine having more Guardian Angel skills! And another charm will look gorgeous on our bracelets!"

Gabrielle found it exciting enough to be a Guardian-Angel-in-training, but what made it even more wonderful was the special charm bracelet that she and all the other Cherubics were given when they joined the school, to which charms were added each time another angelic skill was accomplished. So far Gabrielle had just one pretty charm on her bracelet, but she longed for it to jangle with more and more of them.

As Gabrielle and her friends pottered around Crystals, they chatted about the holidays. While Gabrielle had been back on earth, the others had met a few times in Bliss, the main city in the angel world.

"What did you do when you met up?" Gabrielle asked the others as she began to unpack her things and put them away neatly in her bedside cupboard.

"A bit of shopping..." began Ruth.

"Oh, and we went to this lovely new cafe called Sparkles!" said Hope. "It's such a shame you weren't there too. You'd have loved it."

"That place was a bit *too* sparkly for me," Charity said. "What did you get up to, Gabrielle?"

"Oh…well, it was lovely to be at home with Mum and Dad, but I didn't see as much of my friends as I used to. It's a bit weird now because I don't know any of the teachers at their new school and I can't talk about Angel Academy because it's a secret. I had such a nice time with Grandpa though," said Gabrielle. "And I got my hair cut at the India Rose salon."

"It's so pretty!" said Ruth, admiring Gabrielle's shiny chestnut-brown hair. "You look great. I love your earth clothes. I wish we could wear cool stuff like that here."

"I'm dying to get out of them, actually," admitted Gabrielle. She'd left her home this morning in jeans and her favourite patchwork jacket, but she loved the dresses the angels wore at the Academy.

"Yes, you're all to go to the gown department for a fitting shortly," said Sylvie. "Angel Willow has been working on new creations for you. And it's no secret that they are stunning!"

"Yay! I can't wait to see them." Gabrielle loved the gown department with a passion. Last term she'd spent many happy hours helping Angel Willow with the angel gowns. It had reminded Gabrielle of the cosy sewing sessions she had at home with her mum, and Angel Willow was always very grateful for an extra pair of hands to help put the finishing touches to the intricate gowns the angels wore.

The girls began to tidy their hair and Gabrielle put her halo on for the first time since she'd left for the Christmas holidays.

"That's better!" she said, as she adjusted it in the mirror and it began to glow. "I've missed wearing this."

"I can't imagine what it's like to be without it," said Hope as she touched her own halo. "It's so different for us because we wear ours nearly all the time. Do you still feel like an angel when you don't wear the halo?" she asked curiously.

"Yes, because being an angel is in your heart the whole time, isn't it?" said Gabrielle.

"That's true," agreed Ruth. "Still, I wish you could stay here with us and wear your halo all the time instead of going back to earth for the holidays!"

"If it wasn't for Mum and Dad and Grandpa, I wouldn't really want to go back either," admitted Gabrielle. "Not now that all my best friends are here."

"Come on," said Charity, interrupting anxiously. "There isn't time to chatter. We must go downstairs for the gown fitting!"

"Relax!" said Hope. "There's plenty of time. I want to tell Gabrielle all about the Sparkles cafe. We just have to take you there this term."

"Oh, that's a good idea," said Ruth. "It's amazing, Gabrielle. You'd love it."

"Can't you chat on the way? We can't dilly-dally," said Charity. "It's only a cafe!"

"Come on, then," said Ruth, pulling a face. "I don't think Charity is ever going to relax until we get to the gown department."

Chapter 2

On the way to the gown department, Merry Harper, a friend from the Silverlight dorm, came rushing over to Gabrielle. Merry's hair was longer than Gabrielle recalled and her face glowed, with blush-pink cheeks and sparkly eyes.

"Hey, Gabrielle. It's great to see you!" said Merry, hugging her warmly. "I missed you in the holidays. Did you have a nice time? And how is little Snowdrop?"

"I had a good time, thanks, and she's the cutest. I love her so much!" said Gabrielle. "It was so hard to leave her at home but Mum and Dad will spoil her – they adore her too. How's Anoushka, and the other babies?"

Pets weren't allowed at Angel Academy but Merry had secretly brought her pet rabbit, Anoushka, to school last term and when Anoushka had had babies, Merry had tried to look after them while still keeping it all a secret. She'd almost exhausted herself doing it and Gabrielle and Ruth had tried to help before Merry got into trouble with Madame Seraph, the Head Angel.

"Anoushka's great, thanks!" said Merry, with a broad smile. "I saw some of the babies in the holidays too and they're doing fine."

Once Merry's secret had got out, several of the Cherubics had offered to take a baby rabbit home with them at the start of the holidays, leaving Merry with just Anoushka once more. Gabrielle had fallen in love with little Snowdrop from the moment she'd set eyes on her and had been thrilled to have her as a pet.

"That's great. So it all turned out okay – thank goodness!" Gabrielle replied.

"Yes, I know," said Merry. "I'm going to miss Anoushka this term, but I can see now that Madame Seraph has to stick to the rules. Imagine if we all brought animals to Angel Academy!"

"And we already have our gorgeous

chevalanges here," said Gabrielle. "It was lovely seeing Domino today. I missed him so much in the holidays." Domino was Gabrielle's winged angel horse. Each of the trainee angels had their own chevalange as a partner. It was Domino who'd come to earth this morning to bring Gabrielle back to Cloud Nimbus.

As soon as Gabrielle and her friends reached the beautiful room where the special angel gowns were made, stored and cared for, the angel in charge of the department flew over to them.

"Girls!" cried Angel Willow. "How lovely to see you all!"

"Hello, Angel Willow. It's great to be back," said Gabrielle. "Did you have a nice break? I can't wait to see the spring gowns!"

"I think you'll like them!" said Willow. "Now that I know you all a little better, I've tried to make them in-keeping with your tastes! It wasn't easy, believe me."

Gabrielle noticed that Angel Willow had framed her colour sketches of this season's gowns and hung them near her workstation, so there was a little taster of what was to come. Gabrielle smiled widely – the designs were so pretty, in mouth-watering spring colours, with detailed sketches of lovely pearl beads and satin embroidery.

Angel Willow had already hung the dresses in separate fitting rooms and she ushered the Cherubics into the right cubicles. They disappeared behind a swish of luscious plum velvet curtains and then emerged one by one, wearing gorgeous new gowns in spring pastels of palest pink, lilac, duck-egg blue, lemon yellow and mint green.

"Oh, I totally adore this!" said a delighted Gabrielle, as she appeared in a gown of softest lilac, decorated with beautifully stitched embroidery and glass beads. "I love them all!"

The girls paraded around the  gown department in their new dresses, admiring one another and spotting the little differences that made every one of the dresses unique. They were given a spring cloak and three dresses each for the term and Gabrielle's favourite was pastel pink. "Oh, I know what!" said Gabrielle. "I could save this one to wear on my birthday!"

"Ah, is it your birthday soon then?" asked Angel Willow.

"Yes," said Gabrielle, blushing slightly. "It's in a couple of weeks."

"Cool," said Ruth. "I love birthdays."

"I usually have a really big party at home with all my friends and relatives," said Gabrielle. "But Mum organizes all that. I've never been away from home on my birthday before so I guess it'll be very different this year. But as everything is so perfect here I'm sure my birthday will be—" She stopped as she noticed her friends exchanging looks. "What…?"

"Poor you!" said Ruth. "It's too bad Angel Academy has a rule about no birthday parties at school."

"Does it? Why's that?" asked Gabrielle, trying to hold back a tiny stab of disappointment. She'd imagined birthdays in the angel world would be extra-special somehow.

"Oh, the Governors think there would be too many of them." Ruth's Granny Bell was a school governor and so Ruth often knew things about the school that the others didn't.

"Oh, I see," said Gabrielle. "Now I think of it, there weren't any birthday celebrations in the first term, were there?" She'd been so busy settling into her new life at Angel Academy last term that it hadn't really occurred to her that there had been no birthday parties to go to.

"But that's unfair for you, Gabrielle,"

piped up Hope. "At least we can pop home on our birthday for a party, but it's different for you as your family are back on earth – and I don't think you'd be allowed to go home just for the day and *we* certainly wouldn't be allowed to visit. But we'll get you a cake and we'll all sing to you!"

"And I'm sure you'll get some presents," added Ruth. "And maybe your parents will give you a party in the holidays!"

"That would be nice…" said Gabrielle, thinking that a party with her angel friends would be much better. "And at least I can still wear this beautiful dress on my birthday. That will make it feel special!"

"Of course you can!" agreed Angel Willow.

After saying goodbye, the four angels flew back to Crystals, clutching their gowns and babbling with excitement. Once they'd shown Sylvie their dresses and hung them up in their wardrobes, it was time to get ready for tea.

"I'm so hungry," said Gabrielle. "My mum's cooking is lovely, but the food here is always so delicious." She was also excited to see the Head Angel, Madame Seraph, again. She was magnificent and kindly at the same time, and she always addressed the girls at the first teatime of term, and then each Friday at tea.

As the four friends floated down to the Angel Academy dining room, called the

Ambroserie, Gabrielle could smell the
familiar aromas of warm, freshly baked
bread, buttery potatoes and golden
savoury pies.

"Mmmm, yummy!" she said. "And
something's telling me that pudding's going
to be great too."

"It always is on first day back!" said Ruth
gleefully.

# Chapter 3

As soon as Gabrielle and her friends sat down, Merry came to join them, bringing her friend Fey Lee as well. Their room-mate, Larissa, was chatting to some other friends at another table. The girls gossiped and giggled during the main course about potions, hairstyles and pretty gifts they had received in the holidays.

"Oh look, here comes pudding!" said

Ruth as Angel Patsy, the meal monitor, floated over to their table carrying a tray laden with the most amazing-looking cake. The first pudding of term was a three-tiered chocolate fondant fudge cake, topped with whipped cream, chocolate flakes and butter toffee pieces.

The girls fell silent as they tucked into the dreamy dessert.

"This is almost as delicious as the cake we had at the Sparkles cafe," said Hope after a while.

"Oh, yes. Those cakes were totally awesome!" said Ruth. "They actually sparkled."

"Tell me more about the Sparkles cafe," said Gabrielle. "It sounds amazing."

"Ssshhhh!" said Charity, looking over at

the top table anxiously. "Madame Seraph is going to speak soon. I want to hear the notices!"

"Yes, but she isn't speaking *yet*," giggled Hope. "Stop being such a bore, Charity!" Hope turned to the others. "She's been fussing like this all holiday. Don't you pity me?" she said with a cheeky grin.

Gabrielle noticed that Charity's smile fell and she looked a little cross with her sister. She put an arm around Charity. "We're lucky to have you fussing over us!" she said.

Charity smiled back warmly, clearly relieved to be appreciated by someone.

Madame Seraph disappeared from her seat at the top table where all the teachers ate, and reappeared in the middle of the dining room, hovering there majestically.

Her golden hair cascaded down her back, and her bright blue eyes sparkled. Gabrielle had forgotten just how beautiful and gentle she was, with her exquisitely smooth, dewy skin and rosebud lips.

"Welcome back to Angel Academy, everyone," said Madame Seraph, then she paused, waiting for silence. "I hope you've all had a lovely rest and are ready to commit your time and energy to your angelic training once more. Here at Angel Academy, we are privileged to be preparing you for a very special role – a unique role in the angel community. Becoming a Guardian Angel is hard work, but well worth the effort. Caring for humans calls on our ability to be kind, and I want you to think about that. I want the theme for this term to be about friendship and flowers. If you see a fellow angel feeling sad or left out, then be a good friend, do something to help, take her some flowers, carry out an act of kindness. I trust you all to do this."

Gabrielle smiled as Madame Seraph talked about the importance of kindness. It was the essence of a Guardian Angel's role, after all, and the essence of Madame herself.

Madame continued. "There will be lots of notices to give out on Friday and, of course, we will be announcing our first 'Angel of the Week' for this term. I wonder which of you will be awarded the moonstone brooch?" The sparkling brooch was awarded each Friday to the angel who had stood out during the week as being exceptional for whatever reason. Then the coveted brooch was handed on to the next angel the following week. Madame Seraph smiled as she looked around at the eager young angels. "But for now – good luck, angels!"

Once Madame Seraph had returned to her place at the top table, Hope and Ruth began to chatter again. Soon, their conversation turned back to the Sparkles cafe, which seemed to be at the front of their minds.

"We've got to take you there," Hope said to Gabrielle. "It had the palest pink cupcakes, which actually sparkled!"

"And they tasted as good as they looked," added Ruth.

"And there were glass tables with pink cloths and glittering pink chandeliers hanging from the ceiling!" added Hope.

"And do you remember the mirrors with the cute lights in the powder room?" Ruth asked, grinning at Gabrielle.

"Erm, how could I? I wasn't there," said Gabrielle, suddenly feeling a little left out.

"Oh yeah, silly me. I keep forgetting that," said Ruth, and she turned to Hope. "The little angel lights around the mirrors were like golden halos, weren't they?"

Hope nodded.

It all sounded amazing to Gabrielle, and she longed to go. However, there was no way they'd be allowed down to Bliss at the start of term, so she tried to put it out of her mind for now. Instead she thought about her mum and dad – it seemed like ages ago that she had kissed them goodbye on earth. Could it really have been just that morning? As she flew back to Crystals with her friends, she found herself yawning and decided to have an early night.

Back in the dorm, her eyelids began to droop as she brushed her teeth.

"Night, girls!" said Gabrielle, as she climbed into her fluffy pale blue bed, exhausted but happy. "It's lovely to be back."

"Goodnight, Gabrielle!" replied her room-mates, as they settled down too.

That night, Gabrielle had a strange dream. Her earthly friends were calling out to her from across a river for her to join them and, up above, her angel friends called on her to join them too. But the odd thing was that she couldn't move from where she was; completely stuck between the two groups of friends.

# Chapter 4

The next day was the first Monday of term. By the time Gabrielle woke up, Charity was already up and bustling about in Crystals.

"Morning," Gabrielle mumbled. "You look busy already."

"Hi, I woke really early," said Charity, as Gabrielle sat up and stretched.

As she rubbed her eyes, Gabrielle saw that there were large sheets of paper laid out on Charity's desk, as well as pens, pencils, rulers and multicoloured stickers.

"What are you doing?" she asked curiously.

"Well, I've been thinking it's time we got organized in here so I've made a chart for our chores. Then we'll all know what we've got to do and when," said Charity. "It should stop any arguments."

"Oh, erm, well done!" said Gabrielle, trying to sound pleased.

"Sounds totally horrendous to me!" mumbled Hope from under her bedcovers. "I hate being told what to do, especially by you, Charity."

"It's just a bit of tidying, and fetching flowers, and all the little things we need to do to keep the dorm looking nice. You'll all be glad of my system as the term goes on. Remember how messy it got in here last term when we were all busy?" said Charity briskly. "Come on, it's time to get up now. We don't want to be late on our first day."

"Who said you could order us around?" complained Hope, as she reluctantly swung her legs out of bed.

The twins glared at each other, then seemed to go out of their way to avoid speaking to one another as they got washed and dressed.

After a delicious hot breakfast in the Ambroserie, consisting of scrambled eggs and toasted muffins, washed down with freshly squeezed orange juice, the girls went to their first morning class. This was an introductory session for the term ahead, in which their teacher, Angel Fleur, would give them their new timetables and brief them on what the term's work would cover.

In Angel Fleur's lovely, sunny room there were vases of perfumed lilies on the window ledges and, at each desk, the Cherubics found a "Welcome Back pack" filled with information about their classes, as well as gorgeous pens, pencils and stationery.

"It's all going to be brilliant fun!" Gabrielle whispered to her three friends. "Charity's right – let's make the most of everything by being super-organized this term!"

"I'll organize my own life, thanks very much," muttered Hope under her breath.

As the angels studied their new

timetables they saw that they had some new lessons to go to and some clubs were starting up on Saturdays that they could sign up for if they wished. They also realized Sylvie had been right – for the first two weeks of term, Potion-making was going to take up a lot of their time.

Gabrielle and the other Cherubics had first been taught about potions by Angel Blossom. They'd learned that potions could be created for many reasons – to heal humans, and for extra angelic powers. But this term the Cherubics would be focusing on making a visibility potion. This was so they could complete the Vanishing Charm – last term, Angel Peter, the Vanishing teacher, had taught them how to make vanishing powder, using crystals which

they'd fished from the Vanishing
River, and how to use it to make
themselves invisible. Now he was
going to teach them how to make the
potion which would make them visible
once more.

"Yippee. We go to Potion-making straight
after lunch today!" cried Ruth excitedly as
she studied her new timetable.

"I can't wait!" said Gabrielle.

The potion department was
located in the Angel Academy
gardens, in a perfumed courtyard
by a pretty glasshouse, which
was crammed full of soothing
herbs, such as lavender,
camomile and peppermint.

As Gabrielle approached, she recalled
how nervous she'd been about learning to
vanish last term. She'd eventually got used
to the idea of being invisible, but she was
sure she'd feel more comfortable about it
once they were able to make themselves
visible again. This stage would take the skill
full circle and then they'd be ready to earn
the Vanishing Charm. Charms made all the
hard work worthwhile, as far as Gabrielle
was concerned, and not just because they
looked so pretty. They made the progress
feel real, and the goal of becoming a
Guardian Angel seemed a step closer when
Gabrielle looked at her bracelet.

"Welcome, Cherubics," said Angel
Peter, smiling round at them. "It's lovely
to see you all again. I hope you had a good

holiday and are ready for action! Gather round, please."

Gabrielle noticed that Charity raced to the front of the class with her notebook and pencil, ready to take notes. Meanwhile, Hope and Ruth took their time, giggling as they floated along at the back of the group.

"Last term you all mastered the art of vanishing very well," said their teacher. Gabrielle saw Charity scribbling furiously in her notebook and wondered if she should do the same.

But then Peter noticed too. "Charity," he said kindly, "it's better to listen than to write at this stage. Please put your notebook away."

Looking rather surprised at this, Charity glanced around, then closed her notebook and gave all her attention to the teacher.

Angel Peter continued. "As I was saying, you've all done really well at vanishing and now it's time for you to learn to reappear. Once you can do that, you will sit the final Vanishing Charm test. Vanishing is important because you will need to be invisible during Guardian Angel missions to earth in the future, as you must never be seen by the humans who you will do so much good work for. And when you return to Bliss, you will need to be able to make yourselves visible once more."

Charity twiddled her fingers anxiously. Gabrielle guessed she wanted to write down everything the teacher was saying.

"Now," said Angel Peter, "I'd like you to find a partner so you can help each other out – and because we're an odd number, there will be one group of three. When you've done that, we'll all head into the glasshouse."

Gabrielle looked round for Ruth, as they normally teamed up together, but Ruth had already paired up with Hope. Gabrielle felt a little surprised but they were all friends, of course, so it didn't really matter. As she turned to Charity, Merry came dashing towards her.

"Shall we be partners, Gabrielle?" called Merry. "Fey and Larissa are going to team up together."

"Erm, yeah, sure, that's a good idea," said Gabrielle, looking around at Charity anxiously.

She saw a look of surprise spread across Charity's face. Previously Charity and Hope

had always been partners, and the same
with Gabrielle and Ruth.

"We can be the group of three," called
Gabrielle, beckoning Charity over.

But Charity chose to team up with Fey
and Larissa. She didn't look very happy
about it though.

*Oh dear,* thought Gabrielle. *Perhaps I
should have told Merry that I couldn't partner
her? I hope I haven't upset Charity.*

Chapter 5

When they'd all partnered up, the Cherubics
flew into the glasshouse and gathered round
Angel Peter once more.

"When you began Potion-making with
Angel Blossom, you were given liquid
ingredients to blend together," said Angel
Peter. "Now you are going to use petals and
leaves and learn how to make one of our
most important potions from scratch. To

make the visibility potion it's very important that you have the exact quantities of petals and leaves, and you will need six of everything. Then you need the correct amount of base oil in which to mix the ingredients, and everything needs time to blend together – that's called infusion. Once that's done your potion needs to be strained and poured into a test tube ready for use. First of all, everyone should collect a glass jar and matching lid for mixing and storing your potion while it infuses."

Gabrielle smiled across at Charity as the Cherubics flew over to a shelf filled with glass jars of many different colours, but her room-mate looked the other way. And she didn't seem to be making much of an effort to chat to Larissa and Fey either. Gabrielle remembered what Madame Seraph had said at their first tea about being kind and thoughtful towards your fellow angels and she decided to try her best to cheer up Charity later.

Once they'd selected their jars the Cherubics fluttered around the glasshouse carrying baskets, in search of the delicate, scented petals required for the visibility potion. Gabrielle forgot her worries for a while as she picked orange blossom, rose petals and sprigs of lavender. Then she and Merry flew to a workbench to mix the ingredients, counting out six of everything carefully before stirring.

"Your potions now just need to infuse," explained Angel Peter, "so we'll pop your jars away and they'll be ready in time for your next class with me." They all wrote their names on the labels of their glass potion jars and Angel Peter locked them in a duck-egg blue cool cupboard in the far corner of the glasshouse.

As they prepared to head back up to school, Gabrielle noticed that Charity and Hope seemed to be exchanging cross words, while Ruth stood awkwardly nearby. She flew over and showed her room-mates the little posy she'd made of sprigs and blossoms left over from the lesson. "This lavender has such a lovely fragrance," she said. "It makes me feel so calm!"

"Give some to Charity then," said Hope. "She could do with calming down a bit!"

Silence. No one said a word.

The four girls from Crystals were normally

noisy and chatty, gently teasing each other and making jokes, but they flew back into school quietly. And Gabrielle worried that nothing was quite the same as it had been before the holiday.

Gabrielle had never known Crystals to be as quiet as it was after tea that night, during free time. She decided to use the peace to get on with writing to Mum and Dad. However, she was itching for everyone to do something together – playing a board game or trying out hairdos would have been nice, or even making the room look pretty. Crystals was definitely more fun when everyone was happy and bubbly.

By the first Wednesday of term, everyone was slowly settling into the new timetable

and different lessons, as well as getting
used to the dreaded homework again, but
Gabrielle was keen for some fun. They had
some free time in the middle of the
afternoon, just before tea.

"I think we should decorate our room
with vases of flowers. Or branches of
blossom. It is spring after all. It should be
a joyful time!" she said enthusiastically,
as they all sat on their beds doing their
own thing.

Charity put down the book she was
reading, entitled *Greatest Guardian Angels*.
"That's on my new rota, actually," she said,
with a sigh. She got up and went over to the
colourful chart she'd put up on the dorm
pinboard. "It's Hope's turn to get the flowers
today and your turn next week, Gabrielle…"

Hope sniffed loudly, and carried on reading a magazine about chevalanges.

Ruth was busily shaping her nails. She raised her eyebrows at Gabrielle but said nothing.

"I don't mind doing it this week," said Gabrielle. "Does anyone want to come with me? It's so lovely outside."

But there was no response.

"Ruth?" she asked.

"No, sorry, I've got masses of reading to do," Ruth replied. "After I've finished my nails."

"Well, what about you, Hope?" Gabrielle asked.

"Erm, I'm going to check on Perdita in the stables," said Hope. "I've hardly seen her since we got back." Then she mumbled, "And I'm not doing it if it's on Charity's stupid rota." Although she'd said it under her breath there was a gasp as all three girls heard her. Sylvie hopped about on the windowsill anxiously, but remained silent.

"So, how about you, Charity?" asked Gabrielle.

"No, I'm really not in the mood. Sorry," said Charity flatly.

"Are you okay, Charity?" Gabrielle went over and joined her friend in front of the rota and peered at the neat sheet of chores and who was to do them.

"I'm fine," Charity replied, with a shrug. "I was only trying to be helpful…"

"I'm sure we'll all get used to looking at the rota soon," said Gabrielle, trying to reassure her friend. "But for now I'll go out by myself then," said Gabrielle. "Bye, everyone. Bye, Sylvie!"

"Bye!" called Sylvie, while the others muttered and mumbled, "Yeah, see you later."

Gabrielle took her spring cloak and a pretty basket, and headed out into the corridor. It was lonely with no one to hang out with, and Gabrielle wasn't used to it. *I think I'll see if Merry would like to come,* she decided.

Gabrielle knocked on the door of the Silverlight dorm.

"Hey, Gabrielle! Great to see you!" said Merry when she opened the door. She had such a warm, sunny smile on her face that Gabrielle felt cheered immediately.

"Would you like to come out to the gardens with me? I'm going to pick some flowers for Crystals," said Gabrielle.

"Oooh, yes, I'd love that!" said Merry. "I'll gather some for Silverlight. It'll be fun!"

The two Cherubics flew outside together, side by side. Gabrielle's spirits lifted as she felt the spring breeze on her face and she soared above the gardens, the wind lifting her wings and carrying her along.

"There are some lovely flowers!" Gabrielle called happily, as she spotted a cluster of spring blooms at the edge of the gardens.

Gabrielle and Merry swooped around, flying to the ground whenever they saw pretty flowers to add to their baskets. It was hard for Gabrielle to recall how awkward she'd felt about flying at first. She was nearly as competent now as the angels who'd been doing it all their lives.

"Did you enjoy the first Potion lesson?" asked Gabrielle, as they picked some pretty hollyhocks.

"Oh yeah. I loved it," said Merry. "How about you?"

"It was great! I just love the scent in the glasshouse," said Gabrielle.

"Let's go there and breathe in that lovely perfume once we've got enough flowers," suggested Merry. Although they were not allowed to take flowers from the glasshouse or courtyard for the dorms – as they were strictly for potions – the Cherubics were allowed to go there whenever they liked.

Once their baskets were full, the girls flew towards the Potion-making courtyard.

"How's everything in your dorm this term?" asked Gabrielle.

"Fine, thanks," said Merry. "How about Crystals?"

"Erm, it's not as good as last term," said Gabrielle. "I'm a bit worried about Charity, actually."

"Oh, why's that?" asked Merry.

"She's sort of changed. I can't explain it," said Gabrielle.

"She seemed a bit odd at the Potion-making lesson this morning, I suppose," agreed Merry, "but then it seemed a bit odd that you'd all swapped around too. You usually do everything with Ruth, so I was surprised you were looking for a partner."

They were soon hovering over the pretty courtyard, and the scent of the tangled, sweet-smelling blooms was heavenly, but Gabrielle's bright eyes clouded over when she spotted something odd in the glasshouse. Was she imagining things?

## Chapter 6

Ruth and Hope were in the glasshouse and they seemed to be hard at work. Ruth was stirring a potion in a glass rose bowl, while Hope read from a book and added tiny fragments of petals to the bowl. They looked so busy and happy together, sharing the task, as if they had a joint mission.

"Oh, look," said Merry, "there's Ruth and Hope."

"That's odd," said Gabrielle. "Ruth said she had masses of reading to do. And Hope said she was going to visit Perdita."

"Oh, I wonder what they're doing?" said Merry.

"Yes, I wonder," said Gabrielle.

Gabrielle was surprised and a little hurt that they had not invited her to join them. And to make it even worse, they had refused to come out and help her to collect the flowers, making excuses about why they couldn't come. Had they been planning to go out without her all along? She tried not to get upset and instead imagined what Mum would say if she were there: "Don't jump to conclusions!"

Merry saw immediately that Gabrielle's mood had changed. "There will be a simple explanation," she said reassuringly. "Shall we go and speak to them?"

"No, it's okay," said Gabrielle. "I'd rather not. Let's just take our flowers back to the dorms."

Gabrielle tried to chat to Merry on the way back to school, but all the time her tummy was twisting, as she wondered why her room-mates had left her out. They'd looked like they were having so much fun.

All through tea in the Ambroserie, Gabrielle hoped her friends would mention that they'd been working in the glasshouse. But they didn't.

Later that night in the dorm, as the girls were getting ready for bed, Gabrielle looked in the mirror and took her halo off for a moment, so she could brush through her shoulder-length chestnut-brown hair. She found herself wondering what an angelic hair salon might be like. Sometimes it came over her in a great wave of panic that she was still an outsider at Angel Academy – and in the whole of Cloud Nimbus – and that she might never truly belong in the angel world in the same way the other Cherubics did. Could that be why her friends had left her out?

Hope and Ruth still hadn't said anything about their visit to the glasshouse and Gabrielle couldn't bear the suspense any longer. She cleared her throat apprehensively.

"Erm, what did you all get up to while I was out this afternoon?" she asked.

Ruth and Hope looked at each other and blushed.

"Oh, just my nails, reading and stuff," said Ruth.

"Yeah, stuff," agreed Hope. "Saw Perdita. Groomed her…"

Charity looked on but she just shrugged.

Gabrielle blinked away a tear. She'd seen Ruth and Hope in the glasshouse with her own eyes. Why were they pretending they hadn't been there?

# Chapter 7

Gabrielle threw herself into her schoolwork and on Friday it was time for the first of a whole week of extra art lessons.

"The timetable only says 'special art project' – that doesn't explain much," said Charity.

"We'll soon find out what it is!" said Gabrielle as they floated to the art department, which was like a colourful candy store of paints, pencils, papers, pens, glues and materials. It was another of Gabrielle's favourite places at Angel Academy.

Angel Bellissima, the art teacher, quickly explained that the special project was linked to the Vanishing Charm.

"Before you take the Vanishing test you need to create a locket necklace to hold two tiny test tubes. In one you will keep a small amount of vanishing powder and in the other a measure of your visibility potion," she announced. "You will wear it in the future on Guardian Angel missions to earth."

"Yay!" chorused the girls.

Gabrielle loved Angel Bellissima, with her wild dark hair and big, soulful eyes. She always wore fabulous jewellery, so Gabrielle wasn't surprised she was going to teach them this craft.

"When can we start making them?" asked Ruth impatiently. "I *love* necklaces!" The other Cherubics all nodded enthusiastically.

"Not for a little while!" said Angel Bellissima.

"Why?" groaned Ruth.

"Because we need to create a 'lookbook' first," said the teacher.

"What's a lookbook?" asked Merry.

"The best way to explain it," said Bellissima, "is to show you one!"

The Cherubics all gathered round Angel Bellissima's desk and watched as she pulled a large book from her drawer. Gabrielle was intrigued. It looked like a scrapbook.

"This one is about designing butterfly shoes," explained Bellissima, "whereas yours will be about the locket necklace."

The jacket of the scrapbook was covered with embroidered silk, and inside it was filled with clippings and sketches of flowers and  butterflies, swatches of fabric, flower petals and detailed sketches of the most beautiful butterflies and shoe styles.

"Wow!" gasped Gabrielle. "It's beautiful."

"You see," explained Angel Bellissima, "in order to make a really great job of a design, you have to do lots of research and sketching to get inspiration for it. I want you to think about the vanishing skill – both vanishing and visibility – very carefully and make sketches of all those things you associate with it. Does anyone have any immediate thoughts?"

Gabrielle raised her hand. "Maybe the shimmering vanishing crystal could be part of the design?" she suggested, thinking of the time last term when they'd gone to the Vanishing River to find a crystal to grind down to make their own vanishing powder.

"Bravo, Gabrielle!" said Bellissima. "That's exactly the kind of thing. Anyone else?"

"We'll have to make sure we don't make it too easy to disappear, just by fiddling with your necklace," said Charity, with a frown on her face. "Suppose you opened one of the little test tubes by mistake – you could disappear or appear when you didn't mean to."

While Gabrielle thought that her friend had made a very sensible point, Hope tutted loudly.

"Trust you to think of the risks, Charity," she said.

"No, it's a good idea," said Angel Bellissima.

"I know what!" said Ruth, changing the subject quickly. "We could make matching earrings!"

"Nice thought, Ruth. But Madame does not approve of earrings here at Angel Academy, as you well know!" said the teacher, with a smile. "Okay, girls. Get going on your ideas now. Be as inventive as possible. That is the whole point of design, after all. Good luck, and once you are each happy with your look, we will begin the fine art of jewellery-making!"

It was a lovely lesson. Gabrielle sat with her room-mates and they all chatted, sketched and painted happily, focused on their ideas for their necklaces. It seemed more like old times. Sooner than they could believe, it was lunchtime.

"See you in the Ambroserie," said Ruth. "I'm not quite finished here yet." Ruth was usually the one who finished up quickly, always keen to move onto the next new thing. But today she seemed to be taking ages to pack her things away.

"We could wait for you. I don't mind," said Gabrielle.

"No, no, I don't want you to miss lunch

just because I'm slow. I'll see you in a bit."
Ruth seemed a bit embarrassed, Gabrielle
thought, which was strange because she was
normally so carefree.

"Okay," said Gabrielle. "We'll keep a seat
for you."

Gabrielle floated along to lunch with
Charity and Hope.

"Uh-oh, I forgot to wash my paintbrushes
in art!" Hope suddenly exclaimed, grimacing.
"I'm so dopey, I really am. Be back soon. Will
you keep two seats?" And without waiting for
a reply, she dashed off towards the art
department.

"Okay!" Gabrielle called after her. "We
will!"

Gabrielle nibbled on her lunch of creamy
risotto and crusty bread but Ruth and Hope

seemed to be taking ages to make their way to the Ambroserie. Gabrielle tried so hard not to imagine that they were sharing secrets, as she was sure they must have been doing in the glasshouse. There was a tugging feeling inside her. Where *were* they? She asked Charity where she thought they'd got to, but Charity just shrugged as usual, not in the mood for chatting.

Eventually her other two room-mates came breezing into the Ambroserie together, bubbling over with giggles.

"There you are," said Gabrielle. "I was wondering where you'd got to. I've kept you some of this crusty bread. It's delicious!"

"Oh, erm, thanks," said Ruth. But Gabrielle noticed she put the bread to one side and didn't eat it.

Gabrielle felt confused and finished her lunch as quickly as she could, excusing herself from the table. "I'm just going to pop down to the stables," she said. "I want to check on Domino." She knew she didn't really need to check on her lovely chevalange, but he was so wise that it was always a good idea to talk to him when she felt anxious like she did now.

Chapter 8

She floated back to Crystals to get her cape.

"Hello, Gabrielle," said Sylvie from her perch on the windowsill. "It's unusual to see you on your own. Is everything okay?"

"Yes, more or less," said Gabrielle. She would have loved to tell Sylvie all that was on her mind, but as Sylvie was equally attached to all the room-mates, Gabrielle felt it wasn't fair to explain to the little dove how she was feeling. "I'm going down to see Domino before afternoon lessons."

"That's nice," said Sylvie. "Say hello to him from me. See you later."

As Gabrielle flew down to the stables, her mind was full of thoughts of her cosy bedroom at home on earth. She pictured Mum sitting at the end of her bed on the patchwork quilt, telling her everything would be okay. Her heart ached for a moment as she longed to hug her parents and feel their warmth, and smell her mother's scent of vanilla and roses. Tears sprang to her eyes but she shook them away – she didn't want to cry. Instead she tried to think about the things she was enjoying this term, like designing the locket necklace. And that reminded her how thrilling it would be to add another charm to her bracelet.

Something moving up ahead interrupted her thoughts. To her surprise, she saw it was Charity, flying at great speed.

*I wonder where she's off to?* thought Gabrielle. *She didn't mention at lunch that she was going anywhere – not that she said very much at all.*

Charity flew across the gardens and lawns, then turned towards the lake, speeding down an avenue of blossom trees. Gabrielle watched her for a while.

"How odd," said Gabrielle to herself. "It's not like Charity to fly off on her own." She wondered whether to follow her but there wasn't much time until afternoon lessons and she still really wanted to see Domino.

Domino was in the chevalange paddock, as one of the grooms – who took care of the angel horses when the Cherubics were busy – was finishing off cleaning his stable.

"Hello, Gabrielle!" Domino called in his strong and comforting voice. "Great to see you! How are you?"

Gabrielle flew to Domino and put her arms around his neck. "Hi, Domino, it's so nice to see you!" she said.

"Is everything okay, little one? You don't seem quite yourself today. "

"Yes. Well, no. Well, sort of okay. I'm

probably just imagining things, really. But Charity seems very unhappy. And I think Ruth and Hope are leaving me out of things," she explained.

"How so?" asked Domino.

"Well, I saw them together in the glasshouse the other day but they didn't see me and then later they pretended they'd been doing other things," said Gabrielle.

Domino nodded kindly and waited for her to go on.

"And, well, those two are doing a lot together now. And Charity seems upset about it too, because she and Hope always used to do everything together. But when I've tried to talk to Charity about it, or do things with her, she doesn't seem interested."

"A lot of little worries. I wonder if they are all connected," said Domino, looking thoughtful.

"I don't know. Charity is the biggest of the little worries. In fact, I just saw her fly off on her own. It's not like her. Oh, it all feels different this term," blurted Gabrielle.

"Well now, let's see," said Domino, pausing to think. "Have you quarrelled with any of the girls?"

"No, not exactly," said Gabrielle. "Hope and Charity keep falling out though."

"Perhaps it's just a question of new term blues," he said. "There's always a settling-in period after a holiday. And things don't always stay *exactly* the way you left them."

"I know, that's definitely true," agreed Gabrielle. "When I was thinking about

Angel Academy in the holidays, I assumed we'd all just pick up from where we left off last term. But everyone who lives here did things together while I was away, so I suppose that's part of it."

"It'll be fine. You'll see," said Domino. "The best thing is to be friends with everyone."

"Yes, that's what Mum says and it's what I always try to do," said Gabrielle. "I'll try even harder."

"Good girl," said Domino. "But now it's time for afternoon school," he reminded her gently.

"Thank you for listening." Gabrielle gave Domino one last hug. "Bye for now."

As she flew back up to school for afternoon classes, Gabrielle thought how

lucky she was to have a friend like Domino,
who she could turn to with her troubles.
And this made her wonder again what had
made Charity fly off on her own.

Chapter 9

The next day was Saturday and Gabrielle and her three room-mates were all looking forward to music club, which was a new weekend activity for the spring term. On her arrival at Angel Academy Gabrielle had been delighted to find that she was expected to learn an angelic instrument in her time at the school. She'd been asked to play the flute and was longing to improve, so she was excited about playing in a little group. The club was being led by Angel Lara, who ran the music department and often sang as she walked around the school with a voice as sweet as a songbird's.

In the afternoon, Gabrielle once again found herself on her own, as Ruth and Hope had slipped off somewhere and Charity wanted to finish reading her book. So she went off to help Angel Willow in the gown department for a while, then left in good time for the music club. She arrived ahead of most of the other Cherubics and set up her flute and music stand, then gazed around the department. It was a magnificent space with wonderful acoustics. The high ceiling was painted with beautiful cherubs.

It was especially pretty after dark, as the ceiling was peppered with tiny night lights, which twinkled like stars. There were lots of exquisitely made instruments: baby grand pianos, harps, violins, cellos and, of course, flutes.

The other girls arrived in ones and twos and soon everyone was ready to play. After Angel Lara had welcomed them all, she counted them in.

As they played a piece called "Let's Dance", Gabrielle noticed that Charity, who was sitting opposite her, was becoming agitated. She was playing violin, but every few seconds she stopped playing and shook her head crossly. Gabrielle tried her best to focus on following her own sheet of music, but Charity's behaviour was very distracting.

Some of the others began to stare too. Charity tutted and harrumphed and finally didn't play at all.

When Charity tried to rejoin the piece with her instrument at one point, she played the wrong bar and Angel Lara noticed that something was amiss.

"Please stop there, everyone," called Angel Lara. "Charity seems to be having some problems."

"It's not me who's got the problems," mumbled Charity crossly.

"What's wrong, Charity?" asked Angel Lara patiently. "Did you lose your place?"

"No, I was put off," said Charity.

"Put off?" said the teacher. "Oh dear. In what way?"

"Someone is playing a fraction out of

time," said Charity. "It's someone else on violin. I'm sorry, but it's really putting me off."

"That's a little unkind of you, Charity," Angel Lara told her, "blaming someone else when you made a mistake. There's nothing to be embarrassed about. This is a club. We're here to have fun. Let's pick up again from where we left off."

"No," said Charity. "I won't take the blame when it wasn't me. Someone is playing out of time with the rest of us." She cast her eyes over the violin players and finally settled on one poor Cherubic. "Merry, I'm afraid that I'm quite certain it's you," said Charity matter-of-factly.

"Charity!" Angel Lara exclaimed in shock.

Everyone looked at Merry in surprise. She was a wonderful musician and always had excellent timing. *How could Charity say such a thing?* thought Gabrielle.

Merry put down her violin and looked as if she would dissolve into floods of tears. Angel Lara went over to comfort her.

Charity started muttering under her breath. "Sorry, but someone had to say it."

"Shush, Charity," said Hope. "What's the matter with you?"

"Can everyone please stop staring at me like that?" said Charity, looking flustered. "I didn't mean to be unkind, but it was putting me off."

"Come over here please, Charity," said Angel Lara, as she returned to the front of the group.

Charity floated towards the teacher with her shoulders slumped and her face set in a cross expression.

*Oh no*, thought Gabrielle, *she's only making this worse for herself.*

Hope was furious with her sister.

"Why won't she just let things be?" she whispered under her breath, as Angel Lara spoke quietly to Charity about leaving certain decisions to the teachers.

It was clear to Gabrielle that Charity had annoyed Angel Lara, which was such a pity, because Charity was a very good pupil. *And also*, thought Gabrielle, *music club is meant to be fun.*

"Let's run through it again," said the teacher, "and everyone please follow the notes and spaces a little more closely this time."

Charity went back to her place but refused to play her instrument for the rest of the session.

# Chapter 10

On Monday morning, after a scrumptious breakfast of herb omelettes with buttered brown toast and freshly squeezed orange juice, followed by blueberries with blossom honey and vanilla yogurt, the girls fetched their spring capes and headed to the courtyard for their next visibility Potion-making lesson.

"Gosh, once we can do this, we'll be

ready for the vanishing test," said Gabrielle. "It's unbelievable!"

"Yep," said Ruth. "I hate tests though."

"But once we pass that, we can get the Vanishing Charm," said Hope.

"Ooh, it will be lovely to have another charm!" said Gabrielle.

Angel Peter was waiting for them in the courtyard, and once all the girls had assembled, he addressed the class. Or at least, he tried to. But the Cherubics were in very high spirits that morning. Some giggled, others whispered and another group tried out an Angelfly move they'd learned.

"Cherubics, please concentrate," said Angel Peter, sounding rather cross. "You'll be taking the vanishing test next Monday…" There was a gasp – none of the Cherubics had realized the test was going to be quite so soon. "Although there will be extra lessons this week, as you will see on your timetables, that still doesn't give us long to perfect the potion-making stage."

Gabrielle struggled to conceal her disappointment. "Monday's my birthday," she whispered to Ruth, who stood beside her.

"Poor you! That's such a shame," said Ruth. "Who wants a test on their birthday?"

Gabrielle heard Charity tutting loudly at them and realized Angel Peter was getting steadily more annoyed.

"Gabrielle and Ruth! Have you *quite* finished chatting?" he said.

"Sorry, Angel Peter!" the two Cherubics chorused.

"You still have a lot to learn before the

test, and you will have to work hard," he said. He paced around for a few moments. "Now, you already know how to make the potion, so it's time to strain it into test tubes and then we can move on to showing you how to use it. Can I have a volunteer to help me, please?"

Lots of the girls raised a hand, keen to be picked as Angel Peter's assistant, but none looked keener than Charity. What Charity could not tell the teacher was that she had already successfully brought Ruth back from invisibility last term. Back then they'd been banned from using the visibility potion until they'd been taught how to use it properly, but because Ruth had secretly vanished without permission, they'd had to bring her back to visibility without any of the teachers knowing or she'd have been in terrible trouble.

Now Charity was clearly desperate for some recognition, and Gabrielle thought she deserved it, as she was always making extra effort.

But Angel Peter did not pick Charity as his assistant.

"Larissa, please come forward," he said.

Gabrielle noticed a very sad and lost look coming over Charity's face as Angel Peter, with Larissa at his side, took a jar of potion from the cool cupboard, picked up a sieve and asked Larissa to pour the potion carefully through it into a waiting glass dish.

"You need to strain the potion until it is completely clear," he explained, holding the dish up to the light. "You then need to transfer measures of your potion into test tubes. It's a fiddly job and the potion is potent, so you need to take extreme care."

But even while everyone took out their jars of potion and sieved, strained and poured the liquid into test tubes, there was still a low buzz of chatter and laughter. Only Charity was silent, staring into space.

Angel Peter had, by now, had enough. "Everyone come to the front and gather round!" he commanded, in a tone of voice that the Cherubics had never heard before. They all dropped what they were doing and floated into a huddle to join the teacher at the end of the courtyard, where pink roses grew in perfumed arches, entwined with delicate white jasmine.

"I have never been so disappointed in a

group of Cherubics," he said crossly. "With just a week to go until the test, you are not taking this seriously enough. I have it in my power to cancel the test, and therefore the charm. The Vanishing Charm would be postponed and all your other studies would be affected accordingly."

There was a collective gasp from the Cherubics. If they didn't do the vanishing test and get the charm when they were supposed to, then the next charm would be delayed and the one after that, and they'd always be trying to catch up. Gabrielle for one was completely panicked. All thoughts of feeling sorry for herself because of her birthday clashing with the test dissolved as she realized how much harder they would have to work to get back on track.

After the talking-to they all buckled down and, by the end of the lesson, everyone had successfully produced their own neatly labelled test tubes full of potion, ready to use. Angel Peter seemed pleased with their progress, thank goodness. But as they prepared to fly back up to the Ambroserie for lunch, Gabrielle saw that Charity still looked sad. She went over to her friend.

"What's up, Charity?" she asked softly. "You don't seem yourself. You've not even been updating the chores chart in the dorm lately."

"What's the point? Nobody takes any notice of it anyway."

"But it's not like you to give up. What's the matter?" asked Gabrielle.

"I don't care about anything any more," mumbled Charity. "I'm fed up with school."

"Why?" said Gabrielle, surprised. "You're brilliant at everything at school."

"Face it," said Charity, in a sad, flat voice. "I'm just not popular with the girls, or the teachers. I annoyed Angel Lara and I never get picked for assistant. And you all think I'm fussy and bossy."

"That's nonsense," said Gabrielle. "Everyone likes you!"

"Who?" said Charity.

Gabrielle paused for a split second, but it was long enough to upset Charity further.

"You see?" said Charity with a gulp. "You can't even think of one person!"

"Well, all of us in Crystals, for starters,"

said Gabrielle. "And Merry…" Gabrielle looked away for a moment to wave over to Merry, who was watching her try to comfort Charity.

When she turned back, Charity had gone, flying back up to the school alone. Gabrielle sighed, struck once again by the depth of her friend's sad mood.

Next morning, Gabrielle found herself wondering if there was something she could do to cheer everyone up. Perhaps she could risk organizing a small birthday celebration of some sort. She knew parties weren't allowed at the school but perhaps birthday parties on Cloud Nimbus were very big, grand affairs. If she organized something very small, they might get away with it.

She decided to bring it up in Crystals as everyone was doing their hair and positioning their halos.

"Um, I was thinking," she began, suddenly feeling rather shy, "I know Madame doesn't allow parties, but maybe we could have a little celebration after the vanishing test. It would be lovely to do something for my birthday…"

"Erm, I don't think that's a good idea, Gabrielle," said Ruth, rather quickly. "I think if Angel Peter heard about it he might get the impression that we'd be distracted by the party plans and would neglect the test. You know how he's already threatening to cancel the charm…"

"Yeah, I suppose you're right," said Gabrielle sadly. She had to admit that Angel

Peter had been the crossest she'd ever seen him yesterday.

"I'm not really in the mood for a party," said Charity, not meanly, but sounding fed up.

"Yeah, sorry, Gabrielle. I just don't think it's going to work out, with the test and everything. Bad luck! Rubbish timing," said Hope. "We'll make sure you have a cake though!"

Gabrielle smiled wanly. At least that was one thing in common between earthly and angelic birthdays – the importance of cake.

Sylvie hopped in from the windowsill. "I can't bear to see you all looking so unhappy. We could always have a little tea party in here, just for the five of us," she suggested. "I'm sure Madame Seraph wouldn't mind me organizing that. Then Gabrielle can have a proper party when she goes home for the holidays."

"That does sound nice," said Gabrielle, with a weak smile. "Thank you, Sylvie!"

"Maybe," was all Ruth said.

Chapter 11

Lessons for the vanishing test were getting more frequent and intense. It should have been thrilling, but as she flew down to an extra Potion-making class later that day – a class in which they would actually test out whether or not their carefully-made potions would bring them back from invisibility – Gabrielle found herself daydreaming about how much fun they'd had in Crystals in the first term. She could not imagine that they'd have neglected her birthday in the "old days", which were, in fact, only a few weeks before. *I just don't know why things have changed,* she thought.

Gabrielle and her friends arrived at the courtyard for the lesson, where Angel Peter was itching to get started.

"Once again, I need an assistant," he said. "Hands up, please, if you're willing to help."

Almost every hand shot in the air. Gabrielle didn't put her hand up; she desperately hoped that this time Charity would get picked. But it wasn't to be.

"How about you, Gabrielle?" Angel Peter called. "Come out and help."

Gabrielle edged forward reluctantly, not wanting to seem too keen in case it offended Charity, who'd been bobbing up and down, trying to attract Angel Peter's attention.

"Come on, Gabrielle, quickly now." Angel Peter nodded as she joined him at the front of the class. "Angels," he announced, "I want you to focus. In the vanishing test you will have to show that you can perform all stages of the process from the very beginning. First you will make the visibility potion: pick the petals, mix, stir, infuse, then strain and store – as we've already learned. Then you will use your vanishing *powder* to disappear and the visibility *potion* to reappear, which is what Gabrielle is going to help me demonstrate today. I've brought all your personal vanishing powders from the cupboard in the lab so we can practise the full process from vanishing to visibility. Watch carefully."

Gabrielle felt a bit self-conscious and she looked over to her friends for reassurance. Immediately, she saw the crumpled expression on Charity's face. It pulsed with barely controlled jealousy, and Gabrielle saw a girl – a dear friend – in complete anguish. Charity's expression seemed to say, *But I bought the vanishing book at the Wintervale Fair while the others messed about, and I was the one who brought Ruth back from invisibility, and I always work hardest out of everyone and yet I never get any credit from the teachers.*

Gabrielle had no choice but to do her best and carry out the teacher's instructions, much as she wished she could have swapped places with her friend.

As Gabrielle watched Angel Peter preparing for the demonstration, she recalled how nervous she'd been when she'd first learned about vanishing. She'd tried it a few times since then though, and now she was far more confident.

Angel Peter made Gabrielle disappear by sprinkling a dash of the vanishing powder over her and saying the word "Disparu". She knew she was completely invisible now, yet she felt totally normal. However, it always seemed very odd to her that she could see everyone but they couldn't see her.

Gabrielle stood patiently while Angel Peter asked if anyone had any questions.

"Angel Peter," began Charity, "can you explain why we still have to open doors and windows when we're invisible and can't just walk straight through them?"

"A good question, Charity!" said the teacher. "Even though you cannot be seen by anyone, including yourself, your body is still there," he explained.

*Exactly!* thought Gabrielle, beginning to feel a little neglected. *I'm still here, but you wouldn't know it.*

And on the questions went, back and forth between the Cherubics and their teacher. Eventually, Gabrielle got fed up.

"Excuse me, Angel Peter," she said, "do you think I could become visible again now?"

"Oh, sorry!" said Angel Peter, with an apologetic laugh. "We got a bit carried away there!"

Angel Peter instructed Gabrielle to come and take his hand, then he sprinkled the visibility potion over her, saying "Apparu" as he did so. In a flash, Gabrielle reappeared. *Hurrah!* she thought. Despite Angel Peter almost forgetting her, that seemed to have gone perfectly.

It was time for all the Cherubics to try the whole process.

"Everyone take a partner for this," said Angel Peter. "I want you to make a new batch of potion, as if this was the real test, before you try vanishing and reappearing. And when you get to that stage, make sure that you do exactly what Gabrielle and I did. It's really very simple, but get it wrong and there could be all sorts of problems. Believe me, I've seen everything."

Gabrielle assumed that Ruth and Hope would pair up, so looked immediately towards Charity, hopeful that they could be partners. However, her room-mate looked away moodily. Gabrielle knew she was upset about not being picked to do the demonstration with Angel Peter.

But then, much to Gabrielle's surprise, Hope made a beeline for her sister. *Oh well, at least Charity is going to have a partner today,* thought Gabrielle. *That's good.*

Then Ruth came over and Gabrielle felt her spirits lift as they paired up together for the first time this term. "It'll be so nice to work together," she said. Perhaps everything was returning to normal after all.

"I know," agreed Ruth. "It's about time."

As they started collecting ingredients,

Gabrielle noticed that Hope was a bit giggly, and she overheard Charity saying: "Concentrate, Hope! This is important." But Hope just giggled all the more.

Then, as Gabrielle and Ruth worked away on perfecting their potions, they could hear Charity and Hope constantly niggling at each other.

"Are you sure you're following that recipe *exactly*?" queried Charity. "You can't just guesstimate the amounts, you know. It seems like you're just tearing off petals randomly and throwing them in! That will make the potion work differently from how it should. Angel Peter said six petals! It's six of everything! Let me mix it together!"

"Can you let *me* do this, Charity?" snapped Hope. "You're no good at actually *doing* things – only reading about them and talking about them. I'm the one who gets things done."

Charity tutted crossly, while Gabrielle and Ruth rolled their eyes at one another.

Once the potions had been made, Angel Peter called each pair forward to demonstrate disappearing and reappearing, just as they would do in the test.

"Come on now, girls," he said encouragingly, "this is a very important step towards your final test for the charm. I am expecting great things. I need to see each of you disappear and then reappear again."

Gabrielle and Ruth felt extremely nervous.

"I'll vanish first if you like!" offered Ruth.

"Okay, I'll go after you," said Gabrielle.

The two friends looked over to the twins to see which one was going to be made invisible first. But it sounded as if they had not decided yet.

"You can vanish first," said Hope.

"But I don't *want* to vanish first," protested Charity.

"Maybe we just won't do it at all then!" complained Hope.

"Oh, for goodness' sake," said Charity sullenly. "You win. I'll vanish!"

"I promise it will all go perfectly," said Hope, with a winning smile.

It wasn't the twins' turn yet. But, much to Gabrielle's relief, she and Ruth were one of the first pairs Angel Peter called on.

Gabrielle sprinkled vanishing powder over Ruth, saying "Disparu", and Ruth instantly disappeared. Then Gabrielle instructed her friend to come and take her hand and sprinkled the visibility potion over her, saying "Apparu" as she did. In a flash, Ruth reappeared.

"Well done," said Angel Peter. "With attention to detail, this is such a simple process."

After that, Ruth carried out the whole process on Gabrielle.

"Lovely work, girls," said Angel Peter. "A perfect example of how to do it! Bravo."

As each pair of Cherubics vanished and reappeared successfully, Angel Peter beamed proudly, seemingly much more confident that his Cherubics were shaping up well for their final test.

Soon it was time for Charity and Hope to demonstrate their skills.

Gabrielle watched as they flew to the front of the class. It was plain to see that the girls were still not getting on and Gabrielle began to wonder if it had been a good idea for the twins to pair up together after all.

Much to Gabrielle's relief, when Hope sprinkled the vanishing powder over Charity she disappeared according to plan.

Hope grinned proudly. "And now I shall bring her back with the visibility potion," she said.

"Get a move on then!" they all heard the invisible Charity mutter anxiously.

"Have patience!" said Hope.

As Hope held out her hand for Charity to take, Gabrielle saw Fey make a silly face, which made Hope giggle. As Hope made a face back at Fey, she splashed a dash of the visibility potion in the direction of Charity's voice, and said "Disparu" very quickly.

"Whoa, Hope, slow down, concentrate," said Angel Peter crossly. "You used the wrong word. And you didn't wait to take your sister's hand. How do you know if the potion sprinkled over Charity? You must be much more controlled."

"I knew you'd mess up," snapped the still-invisible Charity.

"You were stressing me!" said Hope between nervous giggles.

As Gabrielle and the other Cherubics watched, Charity began to reappear before them…well, part of her did, at least. One leg emerged, then the other began to materialize – obviously her legs had been splashed with the potion. But it was just her legs; nothing else of Charity appeared. "Look at Charity!" cried Merry. "She's only got legs!"

Gabrielle could see the corners of Hope's mouth twitching as she tried to set her lips in a firm straight line, but she was finding it hard not to laugh, especially as she'd been in a giggly mood all lesson.

As Charity's legs danced around crossly in their red and white stripy tights, some of the other girls also began to laugh. At first, it was just a low hum of gentle giggling. And then a wave of infectious laughter burst through the whole group. But Gabrielle sensed that Charity was not going to be amused.

"Bring back my body!" they heard Charity cry. "And stop laughing at me. It's NOT funny!"

It was obvious from the angle of Charity's legs that she was now flying at full speed towards Hope.

Hope began to fly in the opposite direction and a wild chase developed, with Hope cheekily nipping in and out of Charity's reach, as her sister furiously called out to her.

As Charity squealed in anger, Hope found the situation funnier and funnier. She simply couldn't resist any longer – she let out a little chuckle, then a great long roll of laughter. Soon she was gasping for breath, with tears of laughter rolling down her cheeks.

Angel Peter attempted to take control of the situation. "Girls! Calm down, please!" he cried. "This is a serious situation and our first concern is to get all of Charity back to visibility! How would *you* like to be nothing but a pair of legs?"

His final comment, though designed to make the girls see sense, only amused them more. Even Gabrielle felt it hard to resist the urge to laugh. She was aware that Charity could see everything that was going on, although they could not see her. And Gabrielle knew only too well that it could feel rather weird and worrying when you were invisible, and it must be horrible to know that everyone was laughing at you.

"Girls. Come here at once!" commanded Angel Peter. But neither sister was listening.

"Just you wait till I get a hold of you, Hope Honeychurch," seethed Charity.

"It was an accident!" cried Hope.

"Charity!" Angel Peter commanded again. "Come here this minute." The obedient side of Charity finally triumphed and she did as he said. He took her hand and, saying "Apparu", he sprinkled her with some fresh potion, and brought her back to full visibility.

Everyone stood with bated breath, wondering what Charity would do now.

*Oh please don't go crazy, Charity!* thought Gabrielle. She hated to see her much loved room-mates fighting.

Charity looked down at her body as though checking she was really all there. And just as it seemed she might lunge towards her sister in a rage, she did something unexpected.

Turning to the teacher, she said, "Please may I be excused? I don't feel well."

Angel Peter agreed and she turned away from the whole group and flew quietly back towards the school, with her head hanging low. It was such a sad sight, like watching a wounded bird flying to a place of safety, and to see a fellow Cherubic with her spirit squashed and her wings so limp and lifeless that they barely propelled her forward was utterly heartbreaking. The giggling stopped abruptly and Gabrielle could tell that the other Cherubics also felt suddenly, deeply sorry for Charity.

"Hope, go and see if your sister's okay," urged Angel Peter.

"Oh, okay then," said Hope, trying to look unconcerned, but Gabrielle could tell that her easy-going friend was worried deep down.

With that, Hope raced off to find her sister, leaving Gabrielle and Ruth looking anxiously at one another. It was obvious that the twins were not going to patch up their differences in a hurry.

# Chapter 12

Gabrielle and Ruth got back to Crystals to find the two sisters arguing, while Sylvie fluttered anxiously around them, trying to get them to calm down. Charity hissed at Hope, seething with anger. "Some sister you are!"

"I told you already I didn't mean for it to happen, and you're fine now."

"I'm not fine. Everyone was laughing at me."

"It was funny!" said Hope. "Everybody loved it. Get over it."

"Just…just don't speak to me!" stormed Charity. "I mean it – not a word. If you need to say anything to me, then write it down and I will do the same back!"

Things were not resolved that night, or any time soon after. Gabrielle hated the tense atmosphere over the next few days in the Crystals dorm. Even the thought of her birthday could not cheer her up. As she lay on her bed on the Saturday afternoon, she was surprised when Charity turned to her.

"Will you come outside with me?" she asked.

"Yes, of course, I'd love to," said

Gabrielle, delighted to spend some time
with Charity.

As they took their capes and headed into
the grounds, Gabrielle silently followed

Charity as she flew
towards the lake along
the avenue of blossom
trees that Gabrielle had seen
her fly down a few days
before.

Charity flew to the far side of the lake,
then along the wooded shoreline until she
descended and landed on the veranda of a
dreamy little boathouse, which was tucked
into the trees, overlooking the softly lapping
water. It was painted softest willow-green
and there were several rowing boats
tethered to it, bobbing gently on the lake.

"What a sweet little place!" exclaimed Gabrielle. "I've never noticed it before – how strange."

"I discovered it last week. I love it here," said Charity.

Gabrielle followed her friend through the open door. Inside it was bigger than she'd expected and much more cosy too. There were seats and sofas and lots of shelves of books.

They sat together on one of the sofas.

"How many times have you been here?" asked Gabrielle.

"A few," said Charity. "I come here to think."

"I can see why," said Gabrielle, as she looked out onto the tranquil lake. "It's lovely here. What do you think about?"

"School," said Charity. "I'm not enjoying Angel Academy any more."

"I know," said Gabrielle. "What's changed?"

"Maybe I just realized in the holidays that I'm not the sort of person who enjoys visits to the Sparkles cafe with a whole gang of girls," said Charity. "I don't giggle at silly things or get any of the in-jokes. But I thought, well, at least I am good at school stuff. And I planned to be super-organized and have a really successful term. But it couldn't be going worse. I don't know what to do. If I'm not admired at school and I'm no fun, then what's the point?"

"But, Charity, we've not even been back for two weeks. I promise you this isn't something to worry about," said Gabrielle.

"At least I can come here and enjoy the quietness," said Charity. "And I can cry here without anyone seeing."

"Oh, you poor thing!" gasped Gabrielle, hugging her friend.

"I just can't imagine enjoying school ever again," said Charity.

"Oh, Charity, don't be so sad. Of course you will enjoy it again!" said Gabrielle sympathetically. "Get involved in everything and think positively!"

"I've tried. Really I have," said Charity. "Like with music club. I was trying so hard to make everything perfect but it all went wrong. I really didn't mean to upset Merry, you know," she whispered.

"I know," replied Gabrielle. "But, Charity, things don't always have to be perfect. It's okay to just have fun sometimes."

Charity sighed.

They chatted for a little longer and Gabrielle held Charity's hand as her friend admitted just how fed up she was.

"Perhaps we had better be getting back now?" said Gabrielle softly after a while.

"Yes, I suppose so," agreed Charity reluctantly. "You won't tell anyone about this place, will you?"

"Of course I won't tell. It's our secret."

On the way back to school, Gabrielle and Charity heard the muted sound of lovely music filling the air. It was happy music; music that you could dance to. Initially, it sounded very faint, as if it was being played high up in the school.

"Oh, that sounds lovely!" said Gabrielle. "It sounds like it's coming from the music department."

"I didn't think music club was on until later," said Charity.

They flew into the school and followed the sound through the corridors towards the magnificent music department at the very top of the school.

Huddled at the end of the domed music room was a small group of Cherubics, all playing softly on their instruments, conducted by Angel Lara.

"I don't remember anything about music club being early today. Do you?" whispered Gabrielle to Charity.

"No, I didn't hear about it," said Charity, sounding as confused as Gabrielle. Then she looked mournful. "I expect they didn't want me to come after last week."

Angel Lara and the girls clearly felt a little awkward when they noticed Gabrielle and Charity standing there, as the music came to a bitty end, with some people playing on after others had stopped, until they gradually all petered out.

Ruth and Hope were there and Gabrielle saw them exchange a glance, but she couldn't tell what it meant. They smiled and waved, although Gabrielle thought they blushed a bit too.

"Hi, everyone!" said Gabrielle, with a fake-cheery wave. "Don't stop for us. We'll just listen."

"Oh, Gabrielle! Hi, Charity!" said the teacher. "How lovely to see you both! We wondered where you were. This was just a last-minute thing – we changed the time. Why don't you come on in and join us? Grab your instruments and take a seat…"

Gabrielle found her flute box in the store cupboard, then went and sat down next to Ruth, while Charity took out her violin. Gabrielle looked at the sheet of music on the stand. It simply said: "Celebrations!"

"Hi there," said Ruth, smiling warmly at Gabrielle. "Sorry we couldn't find you to let you know about the time changing. It was all a bit last-minute. We didn't know where you were."

"It's okay," said Gabrielle with a brave smile. It was quite true that no one had known where they were. But why had no one mentioned it earlier? Maybe it really had been a last-minute change.

She took up her instrument, as did Charity, and the band struck up again. It was foot-tapping stuff and, as she concentrated on reading the music, she began to enjoy herself, forgetting her worries for a while.

At the end of music club, Gabrielle and Charity flew back to Crystals together.

"Thanks," said Charity.

"For what?" asked Gabrielle.

"For being a good friend," said Charity.

Gabrielle squeezed her hand. Charity had always seemed so independent, but perhaps she wasn't as strong as she made out.

Ruth and Hope didn't appear back for a while and Charity went to bathe, so Gabrielle had a chat with Sylvie.

"Poor Charity," said Gabrielle. "She's having a bad time this term. I know she might seem strong, but she's quite fragile underneath."

"Sometimes the people who act the strongest are those most in need of support," said Sylvie. "I'm so glad that Charity has you to talk to. You're a good friend to her, Gabrielle."

"The twins weren't like this when we all started here," said Gabrielle.

"Sisters have a great way of falling out and falling in again just as quickly," said Sylvie comfortingly. "You mark my words. This will pass over."

"Oh, I do hope so, Sylvie," said Gabrielle. "It really can't get any worse."

Chapter 13

Even though it was a Sunday, the Cherubics had an extra art session to give them time to finish their locket necklaces. As they carefully added delicate swirls of glitter and beautiful miniature gems to their lockets, they all realized that the test loomed before them. The atmosphere at tea was tense.

In Crystals that evening, the atmosphere was even worse. There was none of the fun chat from last term, but a stony silence instead.

In an attempt to lighten things up, Gabrielle turned to Sylvie. "Do you like our necklaces?" she asked.

"I love them!" said Sylvie. "Let me look properly!"

Sylvie began by looking closely at Gabrielle's necklace, made from the finest spun-silver flowers. "It's exquisite, Gabrielle," she said. "I—"

"I can't find mine!" Charity wailed, frantically searching around on the top of her locker.

She began to throw things around the room, looking under magazines and schoolbooks frantically.

"This is all because no one would stick to

my chart!" she said. "If only we kept this place tidy, things wouldn't go missing!"

"Don't blame other people for your own carelessness," said Hope.

"Careless? I'm not careless," snapped Charity. "What about you? I'll never forgive you for making such a fool out of me – you couldn't be more careless."

Gabrielle couldn't stand it. "Let's help Charity look for her necklace," she suggested.

They all searched around the dorm – even Sylvie.

"Oops, here it is," said Hope casually. "I don't know why it's on my desk."

"You must have put it there!" raged Charity. "You're just trying to make me look stupid again."

"Oh, don't be so ridiculous!" said Hope.

"Well, let me see it anyway," said Sylvie, desperately trying to calm things down, as she flew over to look. "Oh, how lovely!"

But the twins did not stop bickering.

Ruth, who had gone back to quietly reading her magazine, *Halo Hairdos*, tried to sort it out.

"You two are a perfect team when you get along together," she said. "You both have loads of great skills, especially when they're added together."

"Nobody cares about my skills," said Charity. "If I wasn't here, no one would even notice."

"Loads of people care about you," said Ruth.

"I doubt it," muttered Hope.

"Stop being so mean to me!" Charity wailed.

"Well, try to be more fun then," said Hope, as she applied some cherry lip balm.

"Fun? What's the point of fun?" said Charity, throwing herself on her bed and grabbing a textbook.

"Not everything has to be an achievement," said Hope.

Before Charity could reply, Gabrielle cut through the conversation with a plea. "Oh, please be friends. We have a big test tomorrow *and* it's my special day. I don't want people to be sad or angry," she said.

"Well, it's all her fault," said Hope, pointing at Charity.

"I didn't start this," complained Charity.

Gabrielle sighed and caught sight of little Sylvie shaking her head sadly. Part of her longed to get out of the dorm for a few minutes, but she also didn't want to leave until the twins were friends again. Yet it seemed nothing they did would help the twins make up.

"Gabrielle," said Hope. "You don't know how lucky you are being an only child."

Charity looked the opposite way, but Gabrielle thought she was close to exploding.

"Hope, that's a bit mean," said Gabrielle. "I'd love to have a sister like Charity. In fact, you're all like sisters to me and I hate all this fighting."

"Yeah, exactly," agreed Ruth. "I hate it too. Why don't you two patch things up before the test. You're just piling more pressure on yourselves."

Charity shook her head. Gabrielle noticed big, glassy tears forming in the corners of her eyes and felt a new wave of sympathy for Charity.

"See, she's the stubborn one – it's not my fault," said Hope. "She's such a pain!"

Gabrielle gasped. Hope had gone too far this time. Charity began to sob. It was a heartbreaking sound to Gabrielle, especially because Charity usually hated to show her feelings; she was always very much in control. None of the girls had seen her like this before.

"Sylvie…please…ask Madame to call my parents…I want to…go…home!" Charity said between gulping sobs.

Sylvie bobbed up and down on the windowsill in a state of high anxiety.

"Oh, Charity!" said Gabrielle. "There's no need for that. It's just been a bad week, that's all. Let's have a nice cosy night. We can play Scrabble and have hot buttered toast and hot chocolate with marshmallows." Gabrielle held her breath. For a brief moment, it seemed that she had got through to Charity.

Charity dried her eyes, and got up off her bed. All the signs were good. Perhaps she was going to give herself a shake and get on with it. And yet, there was something so stiff about her movements that it seemed to Gabrielle as if Charity was not quite as calm as she was making out.

And Gabrielle was right. Because as she,

Ruth and Hope watched helplessly, Charity suddenly flew out of the window at top speed, almost knocking Sylvie off her perch as she went.

# Chapter 14

"Oh no! Where she's going?" Hope cried.

"We've got to go after her!" said Gabrielle.

The three friends took off and tried to follow Charity, but she was flying super-fast and was way ahead of them – soon she was out of sight in the darkness and they had no choice but to return to Crystals.

"Oh no!" wailed Hope. "This isn't like

her at all. Why was I so horrible…? I miss her already."

Gabrielle felt like telling Hope she had brought this about, but she knew that wouldn't help the situation one bit.

"I didn't mean to say cruel things!" Hope said. "Sisters always say wild stuff to each other they don't mean. I was just really annoyed and she's been so weird lately. I don't think she's a nerd, really I don't. Oh, Charity, *please* come back…" she said, to thin air. Her voice trailed off as she began to sob.

"I think we had better fetch Madame Seraph," said Ruth.

"I'll go!" said Gabrielle.

"Let me come with you," said Sylvie and they flew out of the door and raced along to Madame's study.

Gabrielle knocked on the door anxiously.

"Enter!" called Madame Seraph.

"Oh, Madame!" gasped Gabrielle, her cheeks flushed with concern. "It's Charity! She's flown off!"

"Charity? Whatever has happened?" asked Madame. "She's a model pupil."

"She's been sad for a while," said Gabrielle, "but she and Hope had an argument… I think she might be heading home, but she flew off without saying."

"Oh dear!" said Madame. "Poor Charity. We must find her!"

"Oh, thank you, Madame. Please hurry!" said Gabrielle.

Madame Seraph immediately sent Sylvie to ask senior members of staff to send out a search party to locate Charity. Then she flew with Gabrielle to Crystals, where Ruth and Hope were still staring out of the window in shock.

Madame Seraph embraced Hope. "Don't worry. We will find your sister, you'll see," she said soothingly. "She's probably heading for home. We'll get in touch with your parents to make sure."

"I shouldn't have been so mean to her!" wailed Hope. "It's just that she's so clever and always tries so hard to get everything exactly right, so when she tells me what to do I…I feel a bit stupid, I suppose. And I took it out on her. Oh, I've been so horrible!"

"We all feel bad too," said Gabrielle, putting her arm around her distressed room-mate.

"It's just the opposite of what you'd expect Charity to do," said Ruth sadly, gazing out of the window. "She doesn't even have her cape on. She'll get cold out there."

Madame went away to check up on the search party. Soon Angel Fleur appeared with an update.

"Angel Peter, Angel Raphael and Angel Anna have set off on their chevalanges to find Charity. In the meantime, I must insist that you all go to bed and rest. You are all working towards the next charm and we cannot allow disruption to that, no matter what. So goodnight, girls, and be sure that we will find Charity and she will be back with us soon. And when she returns, we shall take great care to ensure that she is aware of how highly we regard her."

Along with Sylvie, Gabrielle and Ruth did their best to console Hope, who was completely devastated about her sister's disappearance.

"What if something happens to her?" she sobbed.

"They'll find her," said Gabrielle. "And Charity is a sensible girl. She'll not get in danger. You know how clever she is; she thinks everything through."

"She *used* to be sensible," said Hope, shaking her head. "I don't know what's been the matter with her lately. I wish I'd known how bad she was feeling. I thought she was just being a moaner, and feeling a bit sorry for herself. I wouldn't have kept making fun of her if I'd realized there was something truly wrong."

"You girls should try to get some sleep," said Sylvie gently.

"Oh, Sylvie, how are we ever going to be able to concentrate on schoolwork tomorrow? And it's such a big day, with the test," said Ruth, as the three girls changed reluctantly into their nightclothes.

They hardly slept that night. Every so often, one of the three girls would call out from her bed, "Sylvie, any news yet?"

And Sylvie always gave the same reply, "I'll wake you if I hear. Try to sleep."

# Chapter 15

By break of day, Gabrielle felt exhausted; she had barely slept and when daylight started seeping in through the curtains, she realized there was no point in even trying any more. Sylvie was waiting at the bottom of her bed as she stirred and Gabrielle saw her there as soon as she opened her eyes.

"Morning, Sylvie," said Gabrielle. "Any news about Charity? Did she go home?"

"No, apparently not. Her parents are out searching too."

Gabrielle thought for a moment and then decided she had to speak up. "Sylvie, I have an idea where Charity might be." Although Gabrielle had been sworn to secrecy, she knew that finding Charity was more important than keeping her secret right now. "She took me to a little boathouse that she goes to when she's unhappy. If she's not gone home, perhaps she's there. It's just across the lake, beyond the trees, I think. I'd like to go and see."

Sylvie bobbed up and down looking very anxious. "No, I'm sorry, I can't  allow it. The vanishing test is straight after breakfast. You cannot afford to miss it. Let me go. If I find her there you'll be the first to know," she chirped. "Oh…and happy birthday, Gabrielle," she called as she flew off as fast as her little wings could take her.

"Thanks, Sylvie," Gabrielle murmured. She felt very flat. Normally she was brimming over with excitement on her birthday, but not today. She was too worried about Charity.

# Chapter 16

The other two girls were soon up and Ruth and Hope both hugged her.

"Poor you!" Ruth said. "It's such bad luck having a birthday when we're all so worried. Perhaps we should save your presents until we hear Charity is safe – otherwise you won't enjoy them as much. And we'll try to make sure you have a nice day, I promise."

The three girls from Crystals slouched

along to breakfast, wishing they did not have to face the vanishing test. Gabrielle's earlier thoughts about the pretty Vanishing Charm, sparkling like a mini vanishing crystal on her precious bracelet, had disappeared from her mind. All through breakfast, the girls tried to read the expressions on the teachers' faces, to see if there was any news about Charity. A terrible thing had happened, yet life at Angel Academy had to go on…and soon it was time to meet Angel Peter in order to take the test.

Although they were desperately worried, all their studying and practising took over and the Cherubics focused as best they could on the test. Everyone was thinking of Charity as they solemnly collected their petals and leaves, then made their potions. One pair at a time, they robotically went through the vanishing and visibility procedure. Hope worked with Ruth this time, while Gabrielle paired with Merry. The laughter of the potion lesson when Charity had chased Hope seemed unimaginable now.

"Well done, Cherubics," said Angel Peter at the end. "All of you have passed the test, and I must commend you on your hard work and effort. Obviously we are missing one person, so we cannot be too excited about our achievements today. But well done – I am very proud of you."

The Cherubics flew quietly back to school. Ruth and Hope had flown off together again so Gabrielle quickly went to find Sylvie, who was back on her usual perch on the windowsill of Crystals.

"Was I right? Did you find her?" Gabrielle cried.

"I'm sorry, Gabrielle, the boathouse was empty," Sylvie said sadly. "I searched high and low, but Charity can't have gone there."

At lunchtime rumours were swirling around the Ambroserie. Everyone said that Charity still had not been found and that Madame was desperately concerned. Although she was starving, Gabrielle knew she wouldn't be able to eat so she excused herself. "Erm, I'm just going to see if a parcel has arrived from Mum and Dad," she said to the others.

"Okay, we'll save you a seat," said Ruth.

Gabrielle was determined to take a look

in the boathouse herself. She knew Charity loved it there and it seemed the obvious place for her to go. Perhaps Sylvie had missed something. Gabrielle just had to check, so she flew swiftly along the avenue of blossom trees.

The problem was that she hadn't paid much attention when Charity had led her to the boathouse and, in truth, she didn't quite know how to find it. Gabrielle's heart began to sink as she searched and searched, with no luck. She hovered over every break between the clusters of trees, sure she'd see the boathouse beneath her, but it didn't seem to be anywhere. Her plan of finding her friend, talking her round and mending her pain began to seem like nothing more than a silly dream. She was about to give up and turn back when she heard her name being called.

"Gabrielle, Gabrielle! Wait for me, little angel." It was Domino. "I've been searching for Charity, and I saw you just ahead of me. Where are you going?"

"Oh, Domino, I'm so glad to see you. Charity took me to a sweet little boathouse once before – it's somewhere she goes when she's feeling unhappy. I told Sylvie about it, and although she didn't find anything I want to check it out for myself. I'm sure it's where she'll be."

"Ah, I know it. Jump on my back, and I'll take you there."

In seconds Gabrielle looked down and

saw the boathouse nestled amongst the trees. It seemed to Gabrielle that there was a soft, hazy light coming from it. *How beautiful it looks,* she thought. *I'm sure Charity will be in there after all.*

# Chapter 17

Jumping from Domino's back onto the boathouse veranda, Gabrielle looked all around her. Then she stepped in through the door.

Inside the boathouse it was silent. A solitary feather floated before her, as though leading her somewhere. Gabrielle thought back to that very first day she'd come to Angel Academy, when angel feathers had

led her through Featherwing Woods to
Domino.

"Charity," she called softly. "Are you in
here? It's me. Gabrielle."

Gabrielle fluttered around the wooden
house and stopped in the sofa area where
they had sat and chatted before. "Charity…
are you here?" she whispered.

She looked in every corner. There was no
sign of Charity. A shiver of fear ran down
her back. If Charity wasn't here, then where
was she?

Gabrielle was about to leave, but then
she paused. She was sure she could sense
Charity's presence. So she decided to search
around one more time. And then she
spotted a pile of blankets tucked behind one
of the sofas. Going to look more closely,

Gabrielle realized that the tip of a feathery wing was sticking out from the bundle. Gabrielle squeezed between the sofa and the boathouse wall and gently pulled the blankets aside. Underneath was Charity, sleeping soundly.

Gabrielle let out a gasp of delight, which made Charity stir. "It's only me!" said Gabrielle as her friend opened her eyes, looking startled.

When she saw Gabrielle, Charity reached out to her and they held hands for a moment.

"I've come to get you," said Gabrielle gently.

"I'm not coming back to school," croaked Charity, her voice barely audible.

"But you must. *Please* come. We all want

you back where you belong. With us," said Gabrielle.

"I don't know where I belong," said Charity. "I don't want to go home and I don't want to come back to school. I just want to stay here for ever."

"You can't do that," said Gabrielle. "We need you at Angel Academy. You are the one who keeps us in check. And you'll get lonely here, all on your own."

"But you could visit me," said Charity.

Gabrielle smiled. "You know that's crazy talk, don't you?"

"I don't want to come back. Really I don't," said Charity.

"Come on. Please," Gabrielle begged.

Charity still didn't budge.

"Madame is worried out of her mind

about you and a whole search party has been launched. We should let them know you're okay," said Gabrielle. "And as for Hope…"

Charity tensed.

"…Hope's in agony without you."

There was a long silence.

"Well, I suppose you're right. I can't stay here for ever," said Charity softly after a moment.

Gabrielle breathed a sigh of relief.

As the two Cherubics squeezed out from behind the sofa, Gabrielle thought how weak and fragile Charity seemed at this moment, totally unlike the bold and forceful girl she'd been before. And she realized that all Charity wanted was a bit of love and affection. She placed an arm around her shoulder and brushed back her friend's hair from her face, like Mum did to her when she was sad.

"Ready?" Gabrielle asked. Charity took a deep breath and then nodded.

Domino was waiting for them on the veranda. He whinnied softly when he saw Charity but said nothing. Then the three of them launched themselves into the air and flew back to the school together in silence.

Sylvie saw them approach and, within seconds, news travelled round the school that Charity was on her way back. There was a huge cheer of delight when she landed softly on the front lawn alongside Gabrielle.

"I don't want a big fuss!" whispered Charity, looking rather embarrassed.

"But everyone is thrilled to see you," said Gabrielle, and she thought that there was a tiny glimmer of delight in Charity's eyes at the unexpected response to her return.

All the Cherubics huddled round and took turns embracing Charity, which made her smile. Then Hope dashed over and gave her sister the biggest bear hug ever, nearly crushing her wings.

"I'm so sorry, Charity," Hope cried. "I didn't really mean the things I said. I'll make it up to you, I promise."

Madame Seraph had never looked so pleased. Once everyone was inside, she came to Crystals, where she embraced Charity warmly.

"Let's get you some food and we can chat," she said.

Ruth couldn't stop hugging Charity. "I'm so glad you're back!"

Gabrielle thought that the Charity from a few days ago might have been appalled by this display of affection. But this Charity seemed quite different. She was, it seemed to Gabrielle, rather like an icicle slowly defrosting.

There was a knock at the door. It was Angel Patsy, brandishing sandwiches, dainty pies and cakes on a plate the size of a small island. There were little rolls filled with succulent ham and peaches, quiche squares, a crusty loaf spread with creamy butter and jam, cream-filled meringues, as well as endless fondant cakes and slices of chocolate fudge layer cake.

Even more amazing to Gabrielle was

that Charity almost polished it all off, washing everything down with cloudy lemonade.

"I've missed the vanishing test. I must take it now," said  Charity, clearly feeling energized by the delicious food.

"Are you sure you're up to the test, Charity? You could do it tomorrow," said Madame Seraph.

"No, I've trained for it, and I'd like to do it now!" said Charity boldly.

"That's my girl," said Hope. "We'll all come to support you."

Angel Peter was more than delighted to supervise Charity's test. And of course, thanks to all her hard studying, it went perfectly.

"I'd expect nothing less from one of my

finest students," he told Charity with a smile. She beamed with pride.

All the Cherubics had now passed the test – which meant they had each earned the special Vanishing Charm to add to their bracelets. And as everyone finally began to relax and celebrate, the school was filled with the sound of excited chatter and laughter.

Back in Crystals once more, Gabrielle looked at herself in the mirror. She looked rather tired after her sleepless night, and dusty from being in the boathouse.

"Maybe I'll wash and put my best dress on as it's my birthday," she decided.

"That's a good idea," said Ruth. "Hope and I have got to pop out now, but once you're ready, come and meet us in the potion courtyard. There are no more lessons today so we can do some Angelfly moves and just hang out. No tests, no problems. Bliss!"

"Bring Charity," said Hope. "And she needs a wash too!"

"Charming!" said Charity, with a grin.

Sylvie smiled delightedly from the windowsill at the marvellous sight of all her charges being happy together again.

Gabrielle washed, changed her gown and tidied her hair and adjusted her halo. She sprayed rosewater behind her ears and on her wrists. Charity showered and changed too, and Gabrielle and Sylvie exchanged a joyful smile as they heard her singing sweetly in the bathroom. As soon as Charity was ready, they raced along the corridors, dying to join the others in the courtyard.

But when they approached the courtyard, it was strangely silent.

"Have we got this right?" said Gabrielle. "Ruth did say to meet her in the potion courtyard, didn't she?"

Chapter 18

"Where is everyone?" Gabrielle couldn't work out what was going on and Charity looked puzzled too.

"I think we've got this wrong," Gabrielle said. "Perhaps we should go back inside."

But just at that moment...

"Surprise! Happy birthday, Gabrielle!" cried all the Cherubics, jumping out and throwing rose petals in the air. They had been hiding behind the trees and bushes all around the courtyard.

Gabrielle was stunned into silence for a moment.

"My goodness! Is this all for me?" she gasped as she looked around.

There were petals floating everywhere. And now she saw tables of delicious party  food being lifted out from the cool cupboard in the glasshouse by Angel Carmel and Angel Patsy, along with jugs of fruity angel punch. Then the music struck up – played by the  same little band of Cherubics who had been rehearsing in the music room the Saturday that Gabrielle and Charity had felt so left out. And they were playing the "Celebrations" tune.

"This way, Gabrielle," said Ruth, who had just appeared in front of her and seemed to be in charge of the party.

Gabrielle sat on a special angel chair made by the girls and placed in the middle of the courtyard. It looked like a flowery, feathered throne.

"I love it!" gasped Gabrielle gratefully.

She felt so proud as she sat there, with her friends fussing around her. She was spoiled with handmade gifts, soaps, jewellery, iced cakes, praline truffles and scented lip balm. Then Ruth and  Hope presented her with a lovely white box, tied with gold ribbon.

Gabrielle thanked them and began to open it.

"This looks exciting!" she said.

Inside was a lovely glass bottle, decorated with hand-painted petals.

"It's your very own perfume," said Ruth excitedly, "called 'Gabrielle's Gift'. We designed it for you in the glasshouse!"

So *that's* what they had been doing in there!

The potion smelled heavenly. "I adore it!" she cried, hugging her friends.

It all made sense now – Ruth and Hope's secret looks and missions, the feeling of being left out, everything that had unsettled Gabrielle since she had first spotted them in the glasshouse. They had been planning this birthday party for her all term. Gabrielle was thrilled about the effort everyone had made especially for her. It was unbelievable.

After the gift-giving it was time for dancing. Some of the teachers played instruments while all the Cherubics swirled around the courtyard. Gradually, a few of the older girls appeared and joined in and the party doubled up as a celebration of Charity's return. Gabrielle looked over to see how her friend was getting on. And she beamed as she saw that Charity was dancing Angelfly moves with Hope and laughing and joking too.

"Wow! Maybe everything is going to be all right after all," said Gabrielle to Ruth. "It's amazing what birthdays can do!"

It was Friday teatime. The girls had settled down into the school routine once more since the test and the party on Monday.

Gabrielle had written a long letter to her mum and dad telling them all about her surprise birthday party, and thanking them for the wonderful 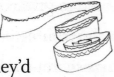 parcel of gifts which they'd  sent. The twins were going out of their way to be nice to each other, and had been allowed to go home for a brief visit after Charity's crisis. Now all the Cherubics were dying to know who would be Angel of the Week, as well as looking forward to a super-delicious Friday pudding.

"This term is starting to be fun at last," Gabrielle said to Ruth as they tucked into a bowl of scrumptious hot creamy soup in the Ambroserie, while waiting for the twins to return from their visit. "Especially now that all the pretending is over!"

"Yeah, sorry about that," said Ruth. "I wanted to give you a lovely surprise party but the trouble is you have to keep so many things secret that it does get a bit difficult. I hope you forgive us!"

"Of course I do," said Gabrielle. "I just felt that things weren't quite right, but I had no idea why. That's when my imagination started making up explanations – even if they were the wrong ones."

"But the party was worth it?" said Ruth.

"Oh yes! Definitely!" exclaimed Gabrielle. "I loved it. I've written to tell my parents all about it. And the perfume is fantastic too! Thanks so much."

"I'm glad," said Ruth.

At that moment, Hope and Charity flew into the Ambroserie, looking rosy-cheeked and giggly.

"Hi, girls!" said Gabrielle. "How was your trip home?"

"It was nice," said Charity. "But I couldn't wait to get back here. Nothing happens at home compared with school!"

"Yes, it's always eventful at Angel Academy, that's for sure," said Ruth, smiling.

"I wonder what pudding will be today," said Hope. "I could do with something extra-special. It's been quite a week. It started badly, then became fabulous, and now it's just nice and normal."

"Yes, we could do with a bit of normal round here," Gabrielle laughed.

At that moment, Angel Carmel brought

out a brand-new type of cake on a three-tiered cake stand.

"That looks awesome," said Ruth. "What flavour do you think it is?"

"I can't tell from here," said Gabrielle, craning her neck to get a better look at the beautiful cake. "But it looks a bit glittery."

One brave Cherubic, Polly, went to ask Angel Carmel what it was. Word spread quickly.

"It's a strawberry meringue sponge cake with SPARKLES!" said Merry as she swung by the Crystals table.

"Maybe Angel Carmel got the idea from the Sparkles cafe," said Ruth excitedly.

"I wonder if we'd be allowed to go there

soon?" said Gabrielle. "I'm longing to try it out."

"I'm sure Madame would allow it, now that this term is settling down a bit," said Ruth. "We'll ask her."

After dessert was demolished, Madame Seraph materialized in the middle of the Ambroserie.

"Well, angels, what a start to the term we've had. But we must always learn from adversity. And I have made a rather unusual decision. We're going to have two Angels of the Week this time, so I have brought another moonstone brooch out of the treasure box. It won't happen again for a while, but this really has been an exceptional week," she said.

All the girls were too polite to urge

Madame to hurry up, but they felt like doing so. They were bursting with curiosity.

"So, without further ado, this week I'd like to award one brooch to Charity Honeychurch for her great courage!"

She paused amidst great cheering and whooping.

"And as for the other," she continued, "I did say at the beginning of term that our theme was friendship. Well, one Cherubic who has displayed devoted friendship is… Gabrielle Divine!"

There was more whooping all round the Ambroserie, but especially from Gabrielle's room-mates.

Gabrielle and Charity linked arms and went forward together to receive their brooches. Gabrielle pinned one on Charity's dress, and Charity pinned the other on Gabrielle's.

"And one final notice," said Madame. "I'm going to allow the Cherubics out of school tomorrow afternoon as a reward for earning their Vanishing Charms. I've booked a large table at the Sparkles cafe!"

"Yippee!" cried Gabrielle, dancing around the Ambroserie hand in hand with Charity. "Angel Academy is the best school in *any* world and this is where I belong!"

## THE END

*Gabrielle loves her life at Angel Academy.*

*If you missed it, discover how she got there in:*

Wings and Wishes

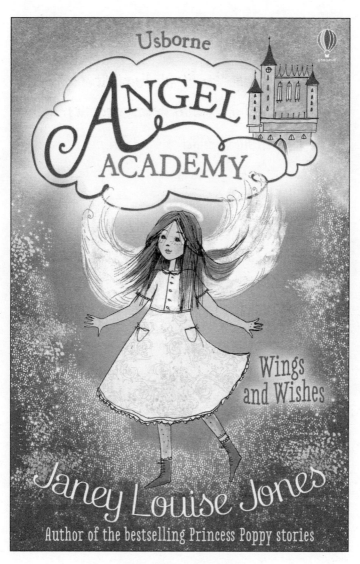

Usborne

ANGEL
ACADEMY

Wings
and Wishes

Janey Louise Jones

Author of the bestselling Princess Poppy stories

ISBN 9781409538608

*It's time for the Wintervale Fair, full of lovely*

*surprises. But why is Gabrielle's angel friend, Merry,*

*acting strangely? Find out in:*

### Secrets and Surprises

Usborne

ANGEL ACADEMY

Secrets and Surprises

Janey Louise Jones

Author of the bestselling Princess Poppy stories

ISBN 9781409538615

If you enjoyed

# ANGEL ACADEMY

you might also like:

## Unicorn Dreams

Lila longs to go to Silverlake Fairy School to learn
about wands, charms and fairy magic – but spoiled
Princess Bee Balm is set on ruining Lila's chances!
Luckily nothing can stop Lila from following
her dreams…

ISBN 9780746076804

# Wands and Charms

It's Lila's first day at Silverlake Fairy School, and she's delighted to receive her first fairy charm and her own wand. But Lila quickly ends up breaking the school rules when bossy Princess Bee Balm gets her into trouble. Could Lila's school days be numbered…?

ISBN 9780746076811

# Ready to Fly

Lila and her friends love learning to fly at Silverlake Fairy School. Their lessons in the Flutter Tower are a little scary but fantastic fun. Then someone plays a trick on Lila and she's grounded. Only Princess Bee Balm would be so mean. But how can Lila prove it?

ISBN 9780746090947

# Stardust Surprise

Stardust is the most magical element in the fairy world. Although the fairies are allowed to experiment with it in lessons, stardust is so powerful that they are forbidden to use it by themselves. But Princess Bee Balm will stop at nothing to boost her magic…

ISBN 9780746076828

# Bugs and Butterflies

Bugs and Butterflies is the magical game played
at Silverlake Fairy School. Lila dreams of being
picked to play for her clan's team, and she's in with
a chance too, until someone starts cheating. Princess
Bee Balm is also being unusually friendly to Lila…
so what's going on?

ISBN 9780746095324

# Dancing Magic

It's the end of term at Silverlake Fairy School,
and Lila and her friends are practising to put on
a spectacular show. There's a wonderful surprise
in store for Lila too – one she didn't dare
dream was possible!

ISBN 9780746095331

For angels, fairies
and more sparkling stories visit:
www.usborne.com/fiction